This World Book Day 20 book is a gift from my local bookseller, Egmont UK and Michael Grant.

D0185423

TO
JACOB!

DEAD OF NIGHT

NIGHT

MICHAEL GRANT

First published in Great Britain in 2017
by Electric Monkey, an imprint of Egmont UK Limited
The Yellow Building, 1 Nicholas Road, London W11 4AN

Dead of Night © 2017 by Michael Grant

I Have No Secrets © 2017 by Penny Joelson

ISBN 978 1 7803 1813 4

A CIP catalogue record for this title is available from the British Library

67255/1

Typeset by AvonDataSet Ltd, Bidford on Avon, Warwickshire
Printed and bound by CPI Group (UK) Ltd, Croydon, CR0 4YY

MIX
Paper
FSC   FSC® C018306

1

'Help! Help, I'm sinking!'

Jillion Magraff is indeed sinking. She is up to her knees in mud and will in short order be up to her thighs.

How Magraff has managed to get quite so stuck is a mystery to Rio Richlin and everyone else in the squad with the possible exception of Sergeant Cole, and that's only because Cole has a very low opinion of the green troops in his squad.

Luther Geer, a big twenty-year-old with a crushing brow beneath buzz-cut brown hair, slings his pack onto a lichen-scarred rock. 'Best just to let her sink. Held up by a woman soldier. Again.'

'Knock it off, Geer,' Rio says, but without much conviction in her voice. Magraff is an embarrassment to all the women in the squad and the platoon. Cat Preeling carries her weight and then some; Jenou Castain . . . well, she has a way to go to become a

1

soldier, but at least she's not quite the whiny, helpless mess Magraff is.

The worst thing is that Rio intensely dislikes Geer, who for his part seems threatened by Rio. So Magraff giving Geer yet another opportunity to sneer at the women in the squad doubly irritates Rio – a sweet-tempered girl who until she joined the army had never had an unkind thought or cast a harsh look at anyone.

At least that's *her* version.

Rio's best friend Jenou would agree that Rio is essentially sweet, generous, kind and certainly innocent. But she would not agree that Rio is incapable of becoming annoyed. No, Rio, in Jenou's estimation, has a stubborn streak a mile wide, and with it just a very slight hint of a temper. That temper came out back at basic training on one of the early occasions when Geer annoyed Rio. Rio marched after him into the men's shower room and demanded his apology. Since then Geer has been just a bit leery of the sweet-tempered milkmaid from northern California, and the incident – Richlin's Raid – has become legendary in the platoon, and Geer has not forgiven Rio.

'Since time began, it was men that went to war,' Geer says. 'And that –' He points at Magraff, then lets his accusing finger drift toward Rio – 'is why.'

The squad are twelve American soldiers with a total of about six months of combat experience, and all that experience – one hundred percent of it – belongs to just one person: Buck Sergeant Jedron Cole. The rest of them are as green as a spring leaf, with a grand total of thirteen weeks basic training each. They are in the zone between civilian and soldier: too heavily armed to be civilians, too ignorant to really be soldiers.

At the moment they are a miserable, cranky bunch, filled with a righteous hatred for the United States Army and the brass hat who scheduled this training exercise for Christmas Eve. They are cold, wet and unless Rio is mistaken, after five hours slogging around in freezing rain followed now by dense fog, quite lost.

'Anyone got any rope?' Geer asks. 'It's not for Magraff, it's for me in case I want to hang myself.'

No rope is to be found. But by tying their webbing belts together they get a line to Magraff who is hauled, weeping and minus one boot, onto dryer ground.

'Beautiful, isn't it?' Jack Stafford joins Rio squatting on a rock while Magraff cleans herself off using a tuft of moss dipped in chilly rainwater as a sponge.

There's a tear in the fog and for a moment it is indeed beautiful, though in a gloomy, oppressive and disturbing way. At least it feels that way to Rio who comes from Sonoma County where it rains seldom and snows never, though she'd have to admit to some fog, especially closer to the Pacific coast.

Steel-gray clouds hang low overhead, a big gray comforter pulled over a rugged country of well-sunken rocks and strange mushrooms, tiny streams, seemingly random stone walls and not a tree to be seen. Puzzled sheep stare from the side of a low hill.

Rio has good eyesight and spots a fantastically antlered deer of some variety a couple hundred yards off. They must not be too far from the coast, she reasons, because a pair of seagulls are riding the breeze overhead, looking down at the squad to estimate its potential for providing food.

'Beautiful,' Rio answers belatedly. 'Bit damp.' Rio's feet are wet and freezing. Her fingers are numb. She can no longer feel her nose and both ears ache. And she's angry at several members of the squad: Magraff for being a helpless nincompoop, Tilo Suarez because he cannot manage to turn off his tedious leering Lothario act and yes, Jenou for draining her own canteen and then begging sips off Rio. She's even irritated at Kerwin Cassel, who she generally likes, because he insists on chewing gum and blowing bubbles and this is meant to be a patrol, not a party.

But mostly, as usual, she's angry at the big hillbilly, Luther Geer.

Christmas Eve? This is Christmas Eve? This foot-soaking, sweaty-cold march to nowhere in full battle dress?

'Damp? Wales?' Jack teases.

'I don't know how you people stand it.'

'Well, *we* don't . . . quite. The south, London, my country, is a veritable desert compared with Wales.'

Jack is the sole Briton in this American army company. Perhaps the only one in the entire US army. He was evacuated from England during the Blitz and in an excess of affection and caution his parents had sent him to live with American relatives in Montana. Sadly, his parents had later been killed by a German bomb and Jack's only way home was to enlist in the US Army as soon as he reached legal age.

Now he is back in Britain and wearing, if not an enemy uniform, not exactly the uniform expected of a boy from Croydon.

He is not terribly tall, just a couple of inches taller than Rio, with ginger hair and the kind of blue eyes that are often amused, just as often devilish, and occasionally, when caught off-guard, touchingly sincere.

'All right, people, off your rear ends, we got some

distance to cover,' Sergeant Cole says. 'That is if everyone can manage not to stumble into quicksand, or break their legs on a rock, or who knows what else.'

They form up, a ragged, muddy, uninspiring bunch. Since arriving from the States, they'd been part of a division that was shuffled from overstuffed camps to rustic bivouacs, marched from borrowed barns to village school houses, on and off the eternal deuce-and-a-half trucks, moving as if the US army has no real idea where to put them or what to do with them. Which, as Cole knows and Rio is starting to figure out, is essentially the truth. The British have been at this war for two years already, but it is all still new to the Americans and they are making it up as they go along.

'Okay, I'm going over this again in the forlorn hope that it may penetrate this time. This little walk in the rain is a squad tactical exercise,' Cole lectures. The word 'squad' and indeed all words containing the letter 's' come out a bit mangled because Sergeant Cole has a nice, fresh new cigar stuck in one corner of his mouth. 'The three elements of the squad are Able, Baker and Charlie.'

Jillion Magraff raises her hand. Like she's in school. Rio knows for a fact that Cole has told Magraff, oh, at least a dozen times not to do that, but rather to simply state her question, but Magraff is not what anyone, anywhere, in any army since Hannibal crossed the Alps, would call a soldier.

'Magraff,' Cole says, rolling his eyes only a little and suppressing a weary sigh.

'Why are they called that?'

'A, B and C,' Rio stage whispers. And adds a silent, *Isn't that obvious?*

Cole says, 'Oh, it's just a matter of preference, Magraff. Would you like to make up some other names? Freddie, Joe and Carmelita, maybe?'

Cole is not usually sarcastic. He is a patient man, a good sergeant. But on this training exercise in a sodden, oppressive landscape in the ass-end of nowhere, with a dozen green soldiers he has already had to pull one soldier (Magraff) out of the mud, stopped another one (Geer) from attempting to shoot down a Merlin, had to backtrack to find a lost rifle (Suarez) and – though he refuses to admit it – become fairly well lost in fog so wet and penetrating he's simultaneously clammy and freezing.

And Magraff only has one boot.

Jesus wept, Cole thinks.

The *usual* American army squad consists of twelve soldiers. The *usual* squad consists of a sergeant, a corporal, and ten privates, all men. This particular squad consists of eight men and four women, because for the first time in American history, thanks to a meddling (to Cole's mind) Supreme Court, women have been made subject to the draft and eligible for enlistment. And because Cole has annoyed his captain by failing to get some paperwork filed in a timely manner, Cole has been given not one, not two, not even three, but four of them. Four women. And, to top it off, an Englishman and some sort of Asian who no one trusts because he sure looks Japanese.

'Able, Baker, Charlie,' Cole repeats. 'A, B, C. It's in the tactical manual which I know you've all committed to memory.'

Eight of the soldiers adopt eight similarly blank expressions meant to convey nothing, but in fact sending the very clear message that no, of course they have not read the manual. The exceptions are Corporal Millican, Sergeant Cole, a serious young man with a prominent widow's peak named Dain Sticklin (inevitably called Stick) and Rio Richlin.

Rio is young and looks younger. She's tall, willowy but strong, with the square shoulders and ropy arms of a hard-working farm girl used to slinging bales of hay, milking cows and shoveling manure. She's pretty but not a beauty, with dark hair, blue eyes and pale skin dotted with freckles. And she has in fact read the manual on small unit tactics. Rio has had serious doubts about her hasty decision to enlist along with her friend, Jenou, but she figures her best chance of coming through it all in one piece is to learn her job.

In fact, she's decided to become a good soldier, and is already a better soldier (in her own inexpert opinion) than anyone in the squad aside from Stick. And Cole, of course.

Rio is quite aware that the Tommies – the British – have a low opinion of American soldiers and are frankly appalled at the very notion of women in uniform. One of the more common snide remarks is that, 'The only problem with the Americans is that they're overpaid, over-sexed and over here.'

The other goes, 'The Yanks are confused – the men fight like women and the women look like men.'

Rio isn't having it. Lord knows she had never planned to be a soldier, but by all that is holy, if she's going to be a soldier she's going to do it well. With her thirteen weeks of basic training, plus two previous training patrols since arriving in Britain, she's pretty confident that she is ready for whatever the army throws at her.

'Able is the command element,' Cole goes on. 'That's whoever is on point, then a rifleman to watch his back and keep track of where we're going, and then the squad leader. That'd be me. Baker is the fire element, that's Stick with his BAR and two others. Whatever is left is the maneuver element, Charlie, in the rear with Corporal Millican there, my assistant squad leader.'

Corporal Millican, in Rio's estimation – and in the estimation of everyone, including Millican himself – is one of those who will never make a good soldier. He's a timid soul with a body to match, though he means well.

Cole says, 'Now, me, I like to mix that up a bit and move a fourth man – or woman, I guess – up front to have that extra rifle behind point, but today we're doing it the O-fficial army way. So, that's how we will proceed to our OB-jective.'

He always pronounces it OB-jective, which invariably makes Rio smile. But not today. Not when she can actually hear the squish of water in her boots. Even the real thing, even combat, can't be any worse than this, she tells herself.

'Our OB-jective,' Cole repeats with a weary sigh, 'which is probably that way. Unless it isn't. Everyone clear?'

They all nod or make murmuring noises.

They move out with Geer on point and Rio just behind him, glancing down from time to time at a compass and a small map. She's been taught basic map-reading skills but nothing on the map matches anything on the ground, and in any event nothing but the ground directly beneath her feet is even visible, because the fog has rolled back in, and it's a fog you could lose an elephant in. She's looking at a map but the closest thing to a landmark is a mossy stone that looks as if someone planted it there shortly after Noah's flood.

Then, through the fog a hazy light.

'Sarge,' Rio calls. 'Is that it?'

Cole joins her and follows the direction of her extended arm.

'Right there,' Rio says. 'If the fog lightens a . . . there! That's a building. It could be a barn, that's what we're looking for isn't it?'

'Can't say it looks much like a barn, more likely a roadhouse, but we're going to pretend it's what we're looking for. So, Stick? You and Baker element – that's you, Pang and Preeling – set up the BAR to provide covering fire, over by that pile of bricks. Charlie element, now is when you come into it: the maneuver element. You're going to head around to the right and turn toward the OB-jective, covering the side and back. Baker and Charlie, you might want to avoid ending up directly in each other's line of fire. Folks tend to resent it when they get accidentally shot by their own buddies.'

The two groups scurry away noisily, bunching up like frightened sheep, tripping over every mound and depression, and Cole thinks, *God help me if I ever have to lead this bunch of fools and schoolgirls into a fight.*

'What do *we* do?' Geer asks.

Rio sees fog swirling around the tall young man's helmet and indulges a momentary fantasy of a great bird descending out of the fog, lifting him up by his rucksack and carrying him away.

'Well, Geer,' Cole says, spitting a piece of tobacco, 'we're gonna wait a few minutes until Baker and Charlie elements are in place . . . and then we are gonna stroll on into that roadhouse and buy a beer.'

'You're sure it's a roadhouse?' Rio asks.

'You got eyes and you got ears and you got fingers. Any other senses, Richlin?'

Rio swallows hard, suddenly back in high school (it's only been a few months) hearing the teacher announce a snap quiz. 'Uh . . . taste? And . . . Um . . .'

'What's in the middle of your face, Richlin?'

Rio, thinking she may have a hanging booger, reaches for her nose and says, 'Oh, right. Smell, Sarge.'

'Now, aside from mold and sheep droppings and Private Geer here, what do you smell?'

Rio inhales, eyes closed. Then opens her eyes. 'Your cigar. And meat.'

'Give the girl a Kewpie doll. Yes, Richlin, roasted mutton, at a guess. If some day, God forbid, you two nitwits end up at the shooting end of this war, remember you can sometimes smell what you can't see. I have not fought me any Krauts yet, but they say you can smell them by their tobacco. Stronger stuff than ours.' He stands up. 'Let's go.'

Within twenty yards it is clear. It is indeed a roadhouse or, as Rio has heard them called, a 'pub'. A carved wooden sign hangs from a wrought iron post above the door.

'The . . .' Rio starts to read, but if the word is English she certainly has never seen its like before. For one thing, there's a hat on the 'w'. 'G-l-y-n-d-ŵ-r Inn. Established 1402. Wow. That's old.'

'As long as they can give us directions,' Cole says, 'I don't care if they're from the Garden of Eden.'

2

The Glyndŵr Inn is a squat two stories and looks a bit squashed, as if it has partly sunk into the earth, whitewash over stone, with an arched, black-painted front door. Cole leads the way inside. As soon as they open the door the smell of roast lamb makes Rio's mouth water. Army food isn't as bad as some folks say, but it is not roast lamb. Beneath the meat aroma comes the yeasty smell of ale, and something sweet, baked apples maybe? Something with cinnamon.

It's a dark, low-ceilinged room, not large but still with a sense that the corners of the room are nearly private spaces. A shallow wooden bench runs halfway around the room against the dark paneling. There's a scattering of tiny round and slightly more capacious square tables, each with the sorts of wooden chairs that have been broken and mended more than once.

The central feature of the room is the bar, a marvel of ancient mahogany with corner moldings carved into sea serpents. The bar top has a thin copper sheet nailed down to form the service surface. Two tall beer taps. Half a dozen bottles of brown whiskey fronting a dim mirror.

The lighting is all by candle – candles on the tables, candles at either end of the bar. And draped above the bar are Christmas lights, tiny colored votive candles dangling from a sagging wire.

A man stands behind the bar. He's old, with gray hair indifferently shoved back from a balding head, and does not look as if he's ever eaten a decent meal. He's all sagging skin over raw bone, rheumy blue eyes and a half-smile revealing more than one missing tooth. But Rio barely notices the barman, because of the young woman standing a few feet away. She has a handkerchief tied around her head, forming bunny ears at the top, like a cartoon version of a person with a toothache, though there's nothing even slightly comic in her demeanor. But more importantly, if her red hair were brown, she would be the spitting image of Rachel Richlin.

Rachel Richlin, Rio's big sister, whose body lies somewhere beneath the Pacific Ocean. Dead at the hands of the Japanese navy.

The ginger woman with Rachel's face stares at Rio

and Rio realizes she's staring back, and of the two of them she, Rio, is the one being rude. She must look very strange, all olive drab, with her (empty) M1 and her (dummy) grenades and her (very heavy) pack and her (soaking) boots.

Rio nods at the woman. The woman just stares.

Sergeant Cole talks to the old publican. 'Evening, sir. My name is Cole, these are my . . . soldiers,' he says, stumbling over the word just a little. 'I don't suppose you could tell us where we are?'

The publican says, 'I imagine I could.' He sticks a glass under the tap and pulls the handle back. Cole watches with very close attention. 'My missus has just now taken a fine roast from the oven. There's plenty for all, and you must be famished.'

He pushes the ale to Cole who looks longingly at it, fights a brief battle with himself, quickly surrenders and gratefully takes the ale. Rio has never been a big beer drinker – or any kind of drinker barring a single incident on the ship coming over from New York – an incident she's trying to forget. But the amber liquid looks good, and as if reading her mind the publican pulls one for her, and for Geer as well, who looks happier than she's ever seen him look.

'Geer,' Cole says, 'Round everyone up. We are

bivouacking here until the fog lifts or the barman closes up.'

'What is your name, miss?' the woman who looks like a younger Rachel asks.

'Me? Um, Private Richlin. And you?' Rio realizes she doesn't know quite what to do with her rifle. The M1 seems particularly out of place in this cozy family-run inn.

'I'm Gwenllian,' the woman says. 'Why were you staring at me?'

'I didn't mean to, it's just that you look exactly like . . . well, like my sister.'

'Of course,' Gwenllian says, as if that makes some kind of sense. 'How many are you?'

It takes Rio a second to parse that, then she blurts, 'Oh, twelve. Twelve of us.'

'I'll tell my mother,' Gwenllian says and turns away.

The rest of the squad comes piling in, vastly increasing the noisiness but also the cheer of the room. They instantly and without asking permission rearrange two of the square and two of the round tables to form one long chow area, and minutes after they complete that bit of work, a pleasantly plump, red-faced woman comes bustling in carrying a massive chunk of roast meat on a pewter platter.

It makes a loud bang as she sets it on a wobbling table. Gwenllian comes behind her with a great bowl of tiny round potatoes and a long crockery dish of leeks and sausages.

Tilo Suarez and Cat Preeling are evidently the only well-raised soldiers in the platoon because they jump up to help, carrying in plates and silverware and bread. The barman keeps the ale flowing and soon a pleasantly full Rio finds a cozy corner from which she can, with just a little stretch, get her soggy boots close to the small fire behind an iron grate. This move does bring her feet perhaps a bit too close to Jack Stafford, who has planted himself nearby, and she has to split the difference between her intense desire to have warm feet and her almost equally intense desire to avoid giving him ideas.

Rio has very little experience with boys or men. She dated once or twice with forgettable boys, and spent some more mature time with Strand Braxton – a boy from home who is now flying B-17s as perhaps the youngest pilot in the USAAF – but a few kisses are the extent of her encounters with men. (Though she did learn a few things during her men's shower room raid.)

Jack Stafford has never been even slightly

inappropriate or forward with Rio, but even an inexperienced girl from the sticks, like she unarguably is, can tell when a man is paying attention. And if this were not the army, and if they were not training for war, Jack might well be the sort of young man who Rio would pay attention to right back. But unlike Jenou, Rio does not see the army as a hunting ground for eligible bachelors.

Cole tells them all to catch some sleep. 'Rule number one: never miss a chance at a hot meal or a warm cot,' Cole says.

Rio is pretty sure Sergeant Cole has more than one 'rule number one,' and in any case she isn't really sleepy.

Gwenllian, unbidden, brings Rio a fresh drink, something warm and spicy, then invites herself to take a seat. For a while the two of them sit in silence and Rio is torn between awkwardness and a deep desire to close her eyes and sleep, soft snoring from Jack encouraging the notion.

Gwenllian leans across the table and says, 'If you don't mind me saying so, you look unhappy, Private Richlin.'

Rio snorts. 'This is not exactly how I was expecting to spend Christmas Eve.'

'I notice you are sitting alone, while your fellow soldiers . . .' She indicates two groups of soldiers chatting, joking, smoking and laughing.

'Soldiers?' Rio laughs. 'We're twelve people with only twenty-three boots between us.'

Gwenllian nods. 'Ah. Like that, is it? Well, Private Richlin, we get many soldiers here. We're a bit of a way station for military folk. Always have been. Soldiers coming, soldiers going . . . soldiers gone.'

An odd turn of phrase, 'soldiers gone,' Rio thinks, and wonders if it was meant to be a joke.

'The whole country is crawling with soldiers,' Rio says.

'Aye, and often has done.'

Rio fights a yawn. 'Please thank your mother for the food. It was wonderful.'

Gwenllian nods, tilts her head and looks carefully at Rio. Then she says, 'You may meet some soldiers this evening. A few of the locals generally pop by. You may hear a few war stories, if you've a mind to listen.'

Rio has nothing to say to this. The food and drink are taking a toll on her senses, and Rachel . . . that is to say, Gwenllian . . . is looking a bit fuzzy around the edges, like a badly-focused photo.

It is then that Rio, thinking of photos, and drifting

from there to memories of Strand Braxton and his camera – the boy loved to take a picture – that she notices that the wall behind the bar, and beside the mirror, is covered with photos, many layers deep. Many of them curl with age.

'Yes,' Gwenllian says, 'In fact, I predict that you'll hear three war stories this evening.'

'Three, huh?' Rio is beginning to think the young woman may be a bit . . . slow.

'Three, yes,' Gwenllian says. 'And may you profit from their stories.'

'Sure,' Rio says noncommittally. In her imagination she's doing the *crazy!* gesture at her temples.

Gwenllian rises, turns toward the door and over her shoulder says, 'In fact, here's George Fisher now.'

Rio looks at the door. No one is there and she decides 'crazy' is more likely than 'slow.' But then, the door opens, and a man walks in.

'Good evening and a Merry Christmas to you, George,' the publican says. He's got a pint already poured and hands it to George.

George is a good-looking man of perhaps twenty-four years, medium height, sandy hair worn shaved at the sides, a bit longer on top. He's wearing what looks like an old military field jacket, a lighter shade of olive drab from Rio's uniform, and muddy boots. Rio thinks it's an enlisted man's uniform: she sees nothing she has to salute. George takes his beer gratefully, sucking the foam from his lip, then surveys the room. There are tables free, but he heads right for Rio.

George nods to Rio and indicates that he'd like to sit at the table, and Rio reluctantly assents.

'George Fisher,' he says and sticks out a hand.

Rio's hand is halfway to his, a polite reflex, when she notices that he has only a thumb and two fingers. She overcomes a momentary hesitation then takes the mangled hand and shakes it. 'Rio Richlin. Private.'

'Ah, good, a soldier not a bloody officer,' George says and sits heavily in the creaking chair. 'So, let me guess: a patrol lost in the fog?'

Rio raises her glass in acknowledgment. It feels like a strangely adult gesture, and she's torn between feeling quite proud of it and wanting to giggle.

'Ah, well, the fog can be friend or foe, eh?' George says.

'Friend?'

He laughs. 'I could tell you a tale . . .'

A tale is the last thing Rio wants, but there's no polite way to say so and Rio – even in her current cranky state – is a polite young woman.

She nods.

'Well,' George says, settling in, 'It's a war story, so I hope you're not overly squeamish.'

'Me?' Rio laughs. 'I'll let you know if I'm offended.'

'Oh, I don't think you'll be *offended*,' George says with a shrewd look. 'Educated, maybe.'

Rio sighs. She wants to be polite, but the last thing she wants is some young Tommy's story that will end with her being made to feel green and foolish. But there is no escape, so she surrenders.

'I'd like to hear it.'

George smiles, but it is not a nice smile. 'Hear it you shall, young woman, but like it? That I doubt.'

3

George Fisher breaks eye contact with Rio, turns slightly to face the fire and says, 'I had some slight experience digging coal and –'

Rio interrupts. 'Cassel . . . Kerwin Cassel over there . . . he's from mining country back in the States.' But George seems not to hear.

'– so I was assigned to the engineers. The tunnelers, to be precise. Me and my mate, Pinky. We've been mates since we was little scrapers, Pinky and me. Of course there were some right bas– . . . sorry miss, my language. But you know how it is. In the army you don't choose your mates, eh? Good with the bad?'

Rio nods, looking at Jillion Magraff, then at Luther Geer. One was an embarrassment, the other was a downright enemy. 'Yes. Good with the bad.'

'Me and Pinky. And Old Will who was a pushy sort, and Alan Crewell a . . . what do you Yanks say? A "gold block"?'

'A gold brick,' Rio corrects. 'Someone who doesn't pull their weight.'

'Ah, that's it. Gold brick. Crewell was a gold brick, all right. And then there was Spellman.' George shakes his head ruefully. 'I hated that git. He was always riding me, always trying to provoke me, him being a London boy who'd learned tunneling working on the underground rails and me a rustic from Ayrshire.' He pauses, blinks, peers at Rio. 'You're not a city girl, I suspect.'

'Me? No, I come from a small town. My mother has dairy cows, my father has a feed store.'

'Yes, you have the look of fresh air about you. As I was saying, I hated Spellman, though I'll admit he worked his plot. He . . . carried his weight.'

He motioned to the publican for a fresh drink.

'The task before us was to dig tunnels beneath the German lines, a quarter of a mile from where we sat. A quarter of a mile of hell above ground. A few hundred yards that had already cost many young men's lives.

'Over on his side Jerry was dug in well, as always. Say what you like about the Hun, he knows how to dig a trench. I inspected a captured Jerry dugout when we took one earlier, and it was very tidy indeed, had a nice plank floor to keep their boots from the mud.

Shelters every few hundred yards, and I mean with lovely solid log roofs and electricity and all.'

'You didn't?'

George's laugh came from a mouth twisted into a wry grin. 'Oh, well, see now, our officers didn't want us getting comfortable. We were meant to attack, you see, to push Jerry back. They figured that if we were nice and dry and comfortable like we'd be reluctant to go over the top and make that run through barbed wire to the German lines. Bloody generals. Not a one of them with any sense, bloody butchers the lot of them.'

George's hazel eyes seemed to have sunk into his head, and were just faint twinkles in darkness. His tone was hard.

'Weeks. Months. The rain was constant of course, and the trenches were full of water, sometimes a foot deep. You'd stand in that water, freezing, and after a while you didn't feel the rot that was eating your soggy flesh away. I saw this one young fellow, too scared he was to take off his boots for fear the Hun would come and he'd have to run shoeless.' He grinned, revealing a missing tooth. He took a deep breath, shook his head slightly and made an effort to appear nonchalant. The effort was not convincing. 'Finally, when he could no longer stand upright, the medicos made him take off his boots and . . . well, the smell . . . There is no smell quite like rotting flesh and gangrene. His feet were swollen, parts white as snow, flesh that sloughed off, just came away as he peeled back his sock. The toes were black of course, black as pitch, dead things still attached. He was sent back to the rear and they took his one foot and three of the toes on the other. And thereby a lesson, young miss: you must always take care for your feet. Your feet are the infantryman's most vital weapon.'

Rio glanced at Sergeant Cole, snoring further down the bench. He'd said the same thing, more than once.

'So anyway, there we were in the mud, the eternal mud of Flanders and some bright spark decided to round up all the fellows with any sort of practical experience and we were to dig a mine from behind our lines, all the way beneath no man's land, to beneath Jerry's pleasant dugouts. Then we were to pack in explosive and blow the bas– . . . I apologize, I have a soldier's tongue, I fear.'

Rio waves off the apology. But she frowns, scrolling mentally through all she knows of this war and finding no references to trenches in Flanders. That seems much more like something from her father's war. But George is far too young to have fought in the Great War, not unless he'd been a newborn infant. He couldn't possibly be more than twenty-five years old at a stretch, and that war had ended in 1918, twenty-five years ago.

'The trick, you see, was not to let Jerry know what we were about. So we had to dig from behind a hill, and sneak the dirt out at night. At first it wasn't so bad. Truth be told, we were happy, Pinky and me, anyway, to be out of the trenches. Once you dig below the slop – the mud – you find, well, more dirt for certain, but solid-packed, you see. And we had pumps to remove the water as well as electric lights and fans to blow air. All the conveniences. And they fed us better, them needing us to work until we dropped every day.'

George's second beer arrived. He took a drink, wiped foam from his mouth and went on. 'Day after day we dug. Pickaxes and shovels, down in that hole. And silent mostly, as silent as we could be, for Jerry is no fool. Jerry knew we'd be likely to mine, so Jerry was counter-mining.'

'Counter-mining?'

'Aye, they dig tunnels hoping to intersect our tunnels.' He leans forward. 'We could hear them. *Scritch scritch scritch.* We could hear them digging. We were like blind men, both sides trying to hide, them trying to find us, us trying to avoid them. Moles, deep in the earth.'

'What did you do if they found your tunnel?'

George shook his head slowly. 'Well, we died more often than not, or had in earlier battles. But we'd learned from that, and now we were quiet as mice. That, and we had learned to dig deep – deeper than Jerry expected.

'Imagine the scene, miss. Me and Pinky and Crewell and Spellman, too, all digging away, our shirts off because it's hot once you get down there. The air stinking of sweat and mold and fresh-cut timber, what air there is.'

'Timber?'

'Well, another crew came behind us, shoring up as we went along. Fresh wood sawn from the forest which had been torn to shreds long since by German artillery. We dug, and we hauled dirt, and we shored up. There were three main tunnels at that time, three long holes in the ground, full of men straining backs and legs and trying not to sneeze lest Jerry overhear and come kill us. We were short-tempered from lack of sleep and lack of sunlight, not that the sun ever shone over Flanders.'

Flanders again. Had the British fought from

trenches in Flanders in this war? Well, obviously yes as to Belgium. The Germans had attacked in 1940 through Belgium which was where Flanders was. Rio made a mental note to ask Stick – he was educated about history.

'Anyway, long story short, though perhaps that ship has sailed, eh? One night I had a terrible row with Spellman. He'd been supposed to bring me fags – cigarettes – which I'd won from him fair and square in a game of cards, and he'd brought only enough for himself.' George looks down at his beer and turns the glass, leaving a ring on the table, but does not drink.

'Bloody stupid row, really. Over nothing. But as I said, none of us were at our best. Tempers short. Men pushed to the limit. I hauled off and hit him with my shovel. Not a deadly blow, mind you, just a smack with the flat side of the blade. I caught him in the nose. Blood everywhere, some of the other lads restraining me, Pinky laughing his fool head off. The worst thing was I'd made it necessary for Spellman to go to the aid station, so we were a man short.'

'How many –' But it's as if George can no longer hear Rio.

'We dug like madmen so as not to earn a punishment. And we were perhaps not as quiet as we might have been.' A look of pain furrowed his brow. 'And all at once, the tunnel just behind me and Pinky, just ten feet back of us, collapsed. Dust everywhere as you can imagine, me and Pinky choking, couldn't even talk, and our first thought was a cave-in. We didn't figure that would be too bad, you see one brace might collapse, but not the whole tunnel.

'But then I aimed my lantern through the dust and saw the hole. A two foot hole in the roof. And a hole, you see, not a cave-in; and that, miss, that was Jerry.'

Despite herself, Rio sits forward. 'What happened?'

George shrugs. 'I saw a hand. I saw a grenade, a Jerry potato masher. What could I do? No time to grab it, nowhere to run, really. Pinky, poor lad, lost his head entirely, was clawing madly at the dirt that had fallen in. The grenade went off and well . . .' For a moment he couldn't go on. He took out a pack of cigarettes, tapped one on the table, and lit it with a shaking match.

'The grenade went off. It went off right between Pinky's legs. Blew his left leg clean off. Mangled the other. And the concussion brought more dirt down on us. Top half of Pinky was buried. The only good thing being that it blocked Jerry's hole, you see, his tunnel collapsing into ours. I heard cursing in

German, muffled. I suppose they were as panicked as we were. Their tunnel had come at ours from an angle, passing just a few feet above us. I don't think they planned it so, it just happened that way.' He sighed, smoked in silence for a moment, eyes distant, seeing things that were not in that pub.

'Pinky...He...I dug him out, still alive, but not for long. I tried to tie off the leg using my belt, but...' He shakes his head. 'Those big arteries in the leg ... well, he was shaking and weeping and calling for his mum. And I was kneeling in mud made of his blood. It took him a while to pass, old Pink. Not a long time by the clock, but it felt very long indeed. All the while, it was just him and me, the two of us, trapped in a pocket no bigger than ...' He looks around the room, searching for an example. 'Well, you see that cubby there where the handsome young man is snoring?'

Rio glances and sees Jack, on a bench, leaned against a corner, one leg out, one curled up, his chin on his chest. Odd. He'd been just a few feet away and she had not seen him get up to leave. Luther Geer is sprawled in a chair with his legs on the bench. Cat, Jenou, Suarez and Kerwin Cassel are across the room having an intense conversation from which the only intelligible words are 'the damn Yankees' and 'the lousy Red Sox'. Sports has never held any interest for Rio, nor for Jenou though she is feigning interest.

'We were in a hole in the ground, miss, a hole no longer a tunnel. The way out was collapsed. My lamp was weakening. The air . . . The thing is, I was relieved when Pinky died at last because I could no longer take his pitiful cries. *Mama. Mama. It hurts, Mum* . . . Calling on his mother and the baby Jesus. But I was also relieved because there was so very little air. He died with a rattle in his throat. And me trying to light him a cigarette, only my match wouldn't catch properly for lack of oxygen.'

He looks at his own cigarette, seeming bemused by it.

'I panicked a bit then. Pinky was my best mate, and me wishing . . .' His mouth formed a crooked smile. 'Wishing in a way that he was dead. Wishing he would get it over and be done with it. But when he was gone, I was alone. Like a rat. Or a worm. I still had my pick and I began swinging away, trying to tunnel up. Of course you can't go straight up, so you go at a slant, but we . . . I . . . was fifty feet down. Fifty feet isn't so much unless it's fifty feet of packed clay. And at a slant it's more like seventy-five feet and there was no possibility of it, really, but what was I to do? It was dig or die. Die digging or die gasping like a landed trout.

'Of course, where I was, I knew even if I made it by some miracle I'd be coming up in no man's land. I knew the minute I took a breath of fresh air there'd be a bullet for me. But I didn't care much, I was like an animal then.'

He fell silent. Drank some of his ale. Lit yet another cigarette.

'But . . . what happened?' Rio asks.

'I dug like a mad thing, miss. I suppose I was truly mad, my faculties all lost, the lack of air, the terror . . . An artillery barrage came down and it was like giants leaping and bounding on the floor above. I dug knowing that success would bring death, but willing to dig and die for a single, final breath of air. And then suddenly I felt the most glorious thing ever in life. Air! Dirt fell into my face, rain fell, but above all: air!'

'You dug through fifty feet?'

'No, miss, I dug less than half that. But I was not . . .' For a moment he struggles to manage his voice. He sucks deep on his cigarette. 'I was not alone. I was not alone. A hand reached down and I took it. A second hand, and I was dragged up out of that hole into a lovely, lovely shell crater. In the middle of no man's land. But there was a man there, a man who had crawled out under the wire with nought but a shovel, and dug like a bloody champion as bullets flew inches over his head and shells landed all around.'

There were tears glistening in his eyes behind the blue smoke.

'Do you know who it was crawled out there, creeping beneath the fog, the lovely fog? Do you know who it was that dug till his back was breaking? Well, miss, that was Corporal Joe Spellman. The man I hated. The man who hated me.'

'But . . . why did he . . .' Rio began before falling into silent confusion.

George leans across the table. 'We were not mates, not in the way that Pinky and me were. But we were mates of a different sort – soldiers of the same regiment. We wore the same uniform.' He nods and smiles shyly. '"Well, George, you lazy git, you been asleep down there?" he asked me. I cursed him, called him a slow-arse for taking his time getting me out. We huddled there in the bottom of that shell crater for an hour or so, me trying to put my wits back together. Luck you see, that crater. Jerry's own artillery had lessened the distance between me and the world above. Then, when the fog had rolled back in, we crawled back to our lines.'

Rio nods. 'Amazing story. You're alive because of him, then?'

George makes a wry face. 'I did not die that day.' He swallows the last of his ale and pushes back from the table, sighing deeply as though he has completed a difficult but necessary task. 'So, there's your war story, miss, and may you profit by it.'

'Can I get you another ale?' Rio offers.

The clock over the bar tolls once. It is 1:00 a.m.

'Thank you, no,' George says. He stands up. 'My time is up. It was a great pleasure meeting you, miss.'

'Likewise,' Rio says, though pleasurable it was not.

She watches him walk away. Only then does she notice the large, dark stain on the back of his uniform. It looks a great deal like blood.

4

Rio sits thinking for a while and gradually begins to suspect that George's story is not entirely truthful. There is nothing new in a soldier embellishing a war story, of course, any more than a fisherman might exaggerate the size or number of fish he's caught. Still, it is disturbing and she makes a mental note to do her best to stay out of tunnels. Also trenches.

She looks around the room, feeling sleepy but not ready for sleep. Jenou is now playing cards with Cat, Geer and Suarez; Sergeant Cole still snores in a corner much like the one Rio occupies. Jillion Magraff draws in a sketch pad. Stick and Cassel and Millican seem almost to be competing to see who can smoke the most. Pang sits alone.

Gwenllian has presumably gone to bed for the night as she is nowhere to be seen.

George could talk all he liked about his mates, but he and they were at least soldiers, Rio tells herself.

To Rio's eye the only soldiers here are Cole and Stick and maybe, just maybe, herself. The rest of them? The only two who'd even bothered to read the manual were her and Stick. The only ones who could hit the broad side of a barn with an M1 were her and Suarez and Stick.

But Rio's greatest annoyance is with the three other women in the squad. After all, their behavior reflects on her; on her and on all female soldiers. None of them had expected to end up here – the assumption had been that they'd be used as typists and drivers. No one had ever imagined that the Army would seriously assign women to actual front line units. But here they are, pretty clearly training for war, for actual shooting war.

Some say George Marshall – that would be Army Chief of Staff George C. Marshall – is sending women into combat to *prove* that they can't take it. Rio has never wanted to go into combat, unlike say Suarez or Geer, who couldn't shut up about how many Krauts they'd kill. But if she were to go to the front line she meant to do her best. She meant to try her hardest. And she did not mean to let herself be judged by low standards set by Jenou, who was from time to time eyeing Suarez speculatively, or by gold brick Magraff sitting there with one boot.

Rio's sergeant back in basic training at Camp Maron had been a woman: Sergeant Mackie. At the end of training, as they were readying to ship out, Mackie had paid Rio a grudging but profound compliment: 'You have potential, Richlin.' That small praise from a woman like Mackie had lit a fire in Rio's heart. She had determined right then not to disappoint Mackie, to earn her respect.

She remembers clearly Mackie walking away, her mirror-polished boots still somehow sinister on the parquet floor.

'I don't even know your first name,' Rio had blurted.

'Sure you do, Richlin. It's Sergeant.'

Rio smiles at the memory. All her life she'd thought she wanted to grow up to be like her big sister, Rachel. Then Rachel had been killed and Mackie had taken that place in Rio's imagination. When she 'grew up,' she wouldn't at all mind being at least a bit like Mackie, first name Sergeant.

There's a sudden loud laugh from Cat Preeling as she lays down a winning hand, and groans from Geer who apparently bet against her. Cat is the only other female in the squad who Rio thinks might amount to something: a big, broad, strong young woman with an easy-going manner and, unlike Jenou, Cat does not spend half her time flirting. Or indeed any of her time.

She glances at Jack Stafford. The Englishman is awake now and writing a letter. She wonders to whom – his parents are both passed. Perhaps he has a girlfriend, in which case he is perhaps not quite as honorable as he might be, eyeing Rio as he does from time to time.

Cat scoops her winnings into her helmet, glances around, spots Rio and walks over to slump into the chair George had occupied all through his long story.

'Well, if it isn't Private Richlin,' Cat says in her wry way. 'All alone in a corner, contemplating the universe no doubt.'

Rio smiles. 'You missed George's story, Cat. You'd have liked it. It was very . . .' She searches for just the right word. 'Spine-tingling.'

'George?'

'The British soldier who was just here.'

Cat looks perplexed. 'Didn't even notice anyone here. Of course, I was busy fleecing those poor suckers. Hah! Geer calls himself a poker player, and I just bluffed him out of half his wages with a pair of deuces and him holding a pair of jacks.'

Rio yawns. 'I don't know what that means, Cat,

but anyone who causes Geer some pain deserves congratulations.'

Cat's grin is about as innocent as her namesake animal eyeing a mouse. 'Why, sweet young Richlin, I should be pleased to introduce you to the intricacies of poker. Assuming you have some cash in your pocket.

Rio yawns again. 'Not tonight. I want to be awake when you clean me out.' She frowns, looking around. 'Have you seen that Rachel . . . I mean that Gwenllian girl? I'm parched and I would love a glass of clean water that didn't come out of a canteen.'

Cat looks perplexed. 'Who?'

'The barmaid I guess she is. The one who looks like my . . . like Rachel, my . . .' She coughs to cover for the lump in her throat.

'Rachel. That was your sister, right? The one who bought it . . .' Cat winces. 'Sorry, Richlin, I am tired and even at my best I'm not always diplomatic.'

'My sister, Rachel,' Rio says. 'It's okay, Cat, okay to mention her.'

'Navy, right?'

Rio nods. 'Japs got her.' She glances at Hansu Pang, eyes narrow with suspicion she knows to be unfair. She's not even sure Pang has Jap blood. Anyway, there had been plenty of Japanese farmers in the area around Gedwell Falls and they'd mostly been hard-working folks who ran their spreads well. Or had until the government rounded them all up after Pearl Harbor.

Still . . .

Cat, following the direction of her gaze, says, 'Pang's all right. Not the worst poker player ever – that'd be Geer.'

'But would you trust him in a tight spot?'

Cat considers. 'I don't know, Richlin. But I guess if we ever do get into the shooting end of the war we'll have no choice but to trust the other guys in the platoon, right?'

Rio shrugs, not committing herself.

'Welp, I gotta find the . . . what do they call it here?'

'The loo?'

'Just the thing,' Cat says, and heaves herself up.

Rio watches her go. Yes, Cat might be okay, though there is something odd about her. Something Rio can't quite put her finger on. But at least she isn't a gold brick like Magraff.

Rio settles back and lets her eyes close, not sleeping, just resting, listening to the conversations around her and the occasional loud exclamations of pain or delight coming from the poker game, and the clinking of glasses being cleaned behind the bar.

She hears rather than sees someone sit down across from her.

'Do you have a light?'

Rio opens her eyes and sees a young woman, almost a girl, holding a cigarette to her lips and looking expectantly at her. She is dressed in layers of mismatched clothing: puffy wool trousers tucked into tall boots that look as if they will fall apart from wear in just another dozen steps, a khaki blouse under a home-knit sweater, all beneath a thick woolen overcoat that looks distinctly military.

'I am sorry, I was rude,' the woman says. 'Would you like a cigarette?' She holds the pack toward her. There's a strange label, not something Rio's seen before. And the woman has a thick accent of some sort, not any of the several British accents Rio has heard so far.

'I don't smoke,' Rio says. But she fishes a Zippo out of her pocket and leans across to light the woman's cigarette.

'I am Tatiana,' the woman says. She puffs, takes a deep lungful of smoke and exhales a blue cloud. 'Thank you.'

'You're welcome,' Rio says.

She stares and realizes after a moment she's being

a bit rude, but the woman does not seem put off. She has blond hair pulled back tight, broad cheekbones and brown eyes. They are serious eyes, sunk deep beneath a broad brow. There's something hungry about the stranger, something spare and hollowed out. Her cheeks are concave, her clothing all loose as though she has shrunk within it.

Or perhaps taken it from someone larger.

'Tatiana. I guess that's not an English name, is it?'

The woman does not smile, but looks at Rio appraisingly, frankly, sizing her up and not looking terribly impressed. That look is intimidating and Rio feels somehow diminished. 'I am Russian,' the woman says at last.

'I'm American,' Rio says.

'Yes, I noticed.'

'You speak English,' Rio says, which is a rather stupid observation but all she can think of.

Tatiana shrugs, and for a moment looks confused. 'It seems I do. I thought perhaps you were speaking Russian.'

'Um . . . No. I don't speak Russian. I suppose you studied English in school?'

Again a shrug, and again a sense that something about this fact is troubling to Tatiana. 'I do not know how I came to speak it. Until this moment I did not know I had your tongue.'

'Are you here for training?'

Tatiana looks around as if only just discovering that she is in a small Welsh pub. 'I do not know why I am here,' she says, 'but I have been many worse places.'

'I guess a lot of us feel that way. Are you a soldier?'

'In a way.'

'Can I . . .' Rio leans forward, excited by the chance meeting with a woman from the only other army known to have women soldiers. 'Can I ask what you do? I don't mean to pry . . . I just don't see many woman soldiers. And you don't look any older than me.'

Tatiana tilts her head, and takes a long moment to reply, a long moment during which Rio again feels judged and not necessarily in a favorable way. At last Tatiana says, 'We are much the same age, but I think that I am much older here.' She touches the spot over her heart. 'I am a soldier, yes, but a partisan. You understand? An irregular. The fascists call us terrorists because we fight them from behind their lines.' She looks down and frowns, noting a medal that hangs from the breast of her coat. It is a small, rectangular red ribbon framed in bronze. From the ribbon hangs a bronze star. 'Ah,' Tatiana says. 'Ah. So.' For a moment her eyes mist over and then she nods slightly, to herself. 'It is like that, then.'

Tatiana holds the cigarette out to look at it, and with a wry smile for Rio says, 'My mother used to tell me that these were bad for me. But I suppose now I can stop worrying.'

Rio doesn't know quite what to say. She knows what she wants to ask, but it will seem incredibly forward and rude. 'Can you tell me . . .'

'You want to know if I have killed.'

Rio is on the point of reflexively denying it, but she nods slowly. 'I suppose I do.'

'It seems I am a Hero of the Soviet Union,' Tatiana says, tapping the medal. 'One does not get one of these baubles without killing.'

She has a sardonic way of speaking, even of holding her head. It is not amusement, quite; that is too superficial a description. It's an expression that combines wry amusement with a deep and gloomy sadness.

It's that sadness that impresses Rio because it is so far from her own irritations and disappointments. There's something dark in the young Russian's eyes and it is different, not just in degree but in kind, from Rio's own emotions. The woman makes Rio feel . . . superficial. Light. Inconsequential. It is an uncomfortable feeling.

Rio thinks, *she's right: we're the same age, but she is so much older.*

'I come from a small village outside Smolensk. We were farmers, of course, what else was there to be? My father took work sometimes as a thatcher . . . that is the word, yes? He put roofs on barns and houses. My mother and my sisters tended the animals.'

Tatiana mimes a motion that Rio knows well and that causes her to break out in her slow-building but dazzling smile. 'You had cows!' Rio says. 'My mother has cows, just a small . . . And I . . .' She then mimes the same milking motion.

'What an extraordinary smile you have,' Tatiana says wistfully. 'May you find it again, after . . .'

Rio wants to ask *after what,* but she's more anxious to hear the Russian's story. 'I'm sorry, I interrupted your story. Please.'

Tatiana shrugs, considers, then without really looking at Rio, but gazing into the swirls of her own smoke, she begins.

'So, as I said, we had a small farm. One day the Germans came. We were not expecting it, it was a . . . how do you say? Surprise?' A small chuckle at that.

'The commissars had told us the Germans would never make it so far. But they did. They rolled up the lane in one truck, six of them in gray. Some were grown men, some mere boys. I even thought one of them was . . . well formed.'

Rio smiles at the odd word choice, but she understands and cannot quite stop her eyes from glancing toward Jack. He is also *well formed*.

'Their leader, a corporal, made motions to explain that he was there to take our cattle. My mother of course said, "No, how can we make cheese, how can we eat, how can we . . ."' She shrugs. 'So, this corporal smashed the butt of his rifle against the side of her head. She fell to the ground. Her . . .' She stroked the side of her own face. '. . . this part, all broken in. My sister, my older sister Valeria, picked up a hoe and was very angry and she is . . . was . . . very fierce.' A gentle smile. A long pause. 'So they stuck her with . . . what is called the knife on the end of a rifle?'

'A bayonet?' Rio asks, telling herself that this can't possibly be what Tatiana means.

'Just so. A bayonet. The German boy, the pretty one, stuck it in her belly.'

'My God!'

Tatiana makes her dry chuckle. 'Your God was not

there that day. I have not seen your God so much lately. Then, of course, they dragged me to our barn and used me.'

'What . . .' Rio swallows hard. She scarcely knows how to think about what Tatiana has said, let alone ask questions.

'They meant to kill me, I think, when they were done, but at that moment an officer, an oberleutnant . . . lieutenant, yes? He came to the farm in a staff car and shouted at them to stop. They took the cows, they took all our food, all we had. Then they burned the house and the barn.' For a moment the mask of wry humor drops and something terrible blazes from Tatiana's eyes. 'And my lovely Valeria . . .'

Rio nods, despite herself. 'My lovely Rachel.'

Tatiana looks at her and for a moment there is a connection so intimate it makes them both uncomfortable, and both look away.

'My mother, her face is broken, and after what happened to me and to Valeria, her soul was broken, too. My father took her to doctors in Smolensk, but now the Germans were everywhere, so he never came back.'

'You were all alone?'

Tatiana nods, but it is less for Rio than for herself.

'I was lucky in one way. I had my monthly visitor, you understand. I was not pregnant from what they had done. But I had no food, and I did not want to leave for fear that my father would return and miss me. And I did not wish to leave Valeria's . . .' She hesitates as if she doesn't know the word, but Rio sees that she simply cannot bring herself to say it.

'Her grave,' Rio supplies.

Tatiana nods. 'Yes. I did not wish to leave her grave.' The word twists Tatiana's mouth. 'But I was so hungry. There were too many Germans on the roads, so I went into the forest. I ate mushrooms I found there. And small green plants, some berries . . . And then, one day I was looking up and there was a man smoking a great pipe and looking at me. He was not so tall, but a big man from here to here.' She indicates her shoulders. 'He was older, of course, like my father, but with fantastic mustaches and deep eyes. And a German machine pistol, a Schmeisser, over his shoulder. And a great long knife strapped to his waist.' She smiles and nods, remembering the moment. 'He looked at me and said, "Little girl, why are you here?" And I told him I was hungry and looking for something to eat. He gave me a piece of bread and a small bite of sausage. I thought he might use me as the Germans had done, and I was so hungry that if . . . But no, he was not like the Germans. He told me his name was Roslov, and I asked, "What is your patronymic and your family name?" And he said, "Commander. Commander Roslov, that is all my name until the last fascist is driven from our Mother Russia."'

Rio tilts her head down to hide the smile that seems inappropriate somehow when speaking to this young woman. Last name Roslov, first name Commander.

Sure you do, Richlin. It's Sergeant.

'Roslov was a major in the Red Army, but detached to help form partisan groups behind German lines. He asked me to tell him all that had happened. I did. How I cried! Sobbing, boo hoo, they killed my sister, they beat my mother. They used me. And do you know what he did, Roslov?'

Rio shakes her head.

'He slapped me. Smack!' The grin is wide this time as Tatiana enjoys Rio's shocked look. 'He slapped me and said, "So what will you do about it, little girl? Will you cry? *Waaah?* Will you lie down in the mud and die of grief?"' Tatiana leans forward and again the wry distance evaporates, the mask slips and something terrible and dark is in her eyes. '"Will you cry, little girl? Or will you hate? Will you hate them, the fascists?"

'And I said, "I would kill them if I could." And Roslov said, "If you hate the fascists I will show you how to kill them."'

Tatiana tapped out another cigarette and lit it with fingers that trembled slightly. 'We were never more than fifty men and woman. Sometimes we were as few as a dozen. We lived in the forest, eating very little, hiding like animals. We wore what we took from the dead. We begged food from farmers who the Germans would kill for helping us. Like animals, but I learned to become a dangerous animal. Comrade Vasiliev was a hunter and he taught me to shoot. My rifle then was not so good, it was from the last war, but I had the eye. I could hit a target.'

Rio cannot help thinking that she, too, is a pretty good shot. But she cannot compare herself to the Russian. Tatiana has been in the war. And even green as she is, Rio knows that there is a line between those who have . . . and those who have not.

'I learned much. There were sometimes classes in history, or in Marxism-Leninism. But mostly I learned to use hand grenades, to shape plastic explosives, to distill poisons from the mushrooms of the forest, to cut telephone wires. To move silently. To use a knife. And each day, Roslov would see me and ask me, "So, Tanyusha," – his name for me – "what have you learned today?" And I would tell him of guns and knives, and he would say, "Have you learned to hate the fascists?" And I would always say, "I need no lessons in hating the murderers of my sister, Comrade Roslov."

"'Ah, but will you kill the fascists, I wonder?"

'And I wondered, too,' Tatiana said. 'I was a good student. Old Vasiliev said I had natural talent at shooting. And one day, Roslov came to me and said, "I have a gift for you, Tanyusha." He handed me a rifle. A rifle with a telescopic sight. It was German Karabiner 98.'

Tatiana smiles in an almost sensual way, savoring the memory. Her hands move gently in the air, carving patterns in the smoke so that Rio can almost see the rifle take shape.

'The fascists make very good weapons. Very accurate, and the best they use as sniper's rifles. I had only two hundred rounds of ammunition. Roslov said, "How many rounds will you use for target practice?" And I said, "Only one tenth. Twenty rounds. Only twenty. That will leave me one hundred and eighty."

"'And how many fascists will you kill with your one hundred and eighty bullets?'

"'One hundred and seventy-nine, Comrade.'

'He was surprised. "Not one hundred and eighty?" He was teasing, you see, because he knew that I had begun to pride myself on my marksmanship. He thought I would say all one hundred and eighty. But I said, "Well, Comrade, I may miss. Once."

'That very night we had a mission. We had intelligence of a German train carrying replacement troops forward. So we marched through the forest all afternoon, long into the night, many miles. We could not ambush the train near any village or the fascists would retaliate and kill everyone as collaborators.

'Just after dawn, at a place where the track curved and began to climb a small hill, we knew it would have to slow down. So it was there that we blew up the track. We derailed the engine. Such a wonderful sight! Smoke billowing and then steam, and such a loud crash!'

Tatiana's grin was feral. 'My place was beside the train, in the woods. I had found a fallen log, very well placed. I was a hundred yards from the track.

The more experienced comrades were closer, but I was untested, and I had specific *skills*, so I was set up where I could see almost all of the train.'

Tatiana mimes her view of the train, holding an invisible rifle, squinting through an invisible telescopic sight.

'The engine was derailed. The next two cars as well, but the rest of the cars remained, and German soldiers, sleepy and confused, came piling out, even though I could hear an officer yelling at them to stay on the train. That officer, you see, he was experienced. He knew it was an ambush. And of course he was right. All my comrades began firing. The fascists were green troops, and they did not at first know what to do, but the officer – he was a Hauptmann, yes? Like a captain in your army. A veteran. He was organizing the men to take cover, to form a counterattack.'

Tatiana leans forward, points her cigarette at Rio and says, 'Never forget, American girl, the German will always counterattack. Yes?'

Rio nods and Tatiana seems satisfied.

'So there he was in my sights. There he was, a handsome man, tall and blond and strong and with a dueling scar on his cheek. A perfect example of the fascist Aryan type.'

Without perhaps meaning to, Tatiana begins to touch the rifle in the air, to hold it against her cheek, to tilt her head slightly to the right, to close her left eye. Her finger curls around an invisible trigger.

'Did you . . . ?' Rio bursts out.

'I aimed. And I thought of those animals . . . and my sister . . . and yet, to take a life . . . To see a man, to see his face, his *eyes* . . . And I knew that Roslov was right. To shoot that man and steal his life . . . Well, my American friend, it was the hate that squeezed the trigger . . .'

Rio holds her breath.

'Bang,' Tatiana says without emphasis. She shrugs and exhales loudly. 'My first kill. I killed four more that day, hate guiding my eye and my hands. Later, Roslov came to me and said, "So, Tanyusha, how many bullets do you have left?"

'I said, "I spent twenty on target practice. And five tonight."

'"How many times did you miss, Tanyusha?"

'"I fired five times, Comrade Commander, and five fascists lie dead."

'He said, "You have done well."

'I was so proud. Roslov said, "Some day you may waste that one bullet."

'And I said, "Perhaps, Comrade. But not today."'

Tatiana sits back, relaxing into the chair. 'Twenty-nine times I fired my lovely German rifle at the fascists, and twenty-nine died. They died for Valeria, and for my mother, and for my father who I learned had been killed in an artillery barrage. They died for all the Germans had done to me, and to Mother Russia. They died but my hatred never slackened.'

'Did you ever miss?' Rio asks, breathless.

Tatiana smiles. 'One day we stumbled into a German force. It was a surprise. We were walking toward a village to see about getting bread and suddenly a whole platoon of German infantry is in the road. These were not green troops. They quickly began firing and so did we but the Germans had cover and we had only the thin trunks of new saplings.

'I fired and a fascist died. Thirty. I fired again, and another died. Thirty-one. And then, I saw what I had never seen before, peering through my sights: it was the mirror image of my own Karabiner 98. And it, too, had the telescopic sight. I was looking at a sniper, like me.'

'Did you get him?'

Tatiana smiles. 'Yes. My bullet took him right in the forehead.' She taps her own forehead lightly.

'But he, too, fired, and because of that my finger squeezed again on the trigger . . . and that one bullet flew who knows where? Up into the sky? But his final bullet, the one he had fired at me, that bullet did not miss.'

Rio shakes her head, confused. 'But . . .'

And that is when Tatiana closes her eyes. Closes them, lowers her head momentarily, almost like an actor at the end of an oration. Then she raises her face and Rio screams.

Screams because when Tatiana opens her eyes again, she has only one. The other is a black pit without an eyeball.

Tatiana seems amused by Rio's reaction. She stubs out her tiny butt of cigarette. She stands heavily and says, 'Yes, it is a shock to me as well. And now . . .' She taps the medal on her chest. 'It seems I am a hero. And like so many heroes, one who will fight no more. May you have better fortune, Rio Richlin who has come far from Gedwell Falls, California, to fight the fascists.'

It barely registers on Rio's consciousness that she has not told Tatiana where she is from. Rio can see nothing but that terrible, empty eye socket.

Tatiana stands, pulls her coat around her, and turns

away, and now Rio sees the dry blood and matted hair and shards of bone from the exit wound that has blown out the back of Tatiana's skull.

Tatiana turns back, and her lost eye is back where it should be, and her expression is once again wry. 'Thirty-two, my American friend. I think when you have learned to hate you may exceed my number.'

5

'What the hell, Richlin? You have a nightmare or something?'

It's Geer, looming up over her. He's half drunk, weaving slightly, a long-ashed cigarette dangling forgotten in his hand.

For a moment Rio cannot answer. Her body feels electrified. It feels as if ants are crawling across her flesh. The image of that empty eye socket, joining the memory of George's blood-soaked coat, has her feeling as if she's losing her mind.

'Leave me alone, Geer.'

'You gonna scream like that when the Krauts start shooting?'

'I said leave me alone.' Fear adds ferocity to her dismissal.

Geer snorts. 'Awww, is the mighty Richlin starting to go a little looney tunes?'

'Get off her back, Geer.' This comes from Jack.

Rio snaps her head sideways and glares at him now. 'I don't need any help dealing with Geer,' she says coldly.

Jack recoils, frowns and subsides in a pout. Rio regrets snapping at Jack, but she has to make it clear that she stands on her own two feet and carries her own weight. Whatever sort of vague chivalry Jack thinks he's practicing has no place in the squad.

Geer laughs. 'Well, try to not to scream any more, huh, Richlin? I'm getting ready to sack out.'

Geer leaves and Rio considers apologizing to Jack, but no, however much she may have hurt Jack's feelings, she will not have him – or anyone – stick up for her as if she's the school goat being picked on by some bully.

Just a nightmare.

Two nightmares, she tells herself. Nothing more. The result of a tired brain and abused body. *Well*, she thinks, *at least I'm too jazzed now to fall asleep, so no more nightmares.*

'I'm going to get some fresh air,' she says to Jack. He seems on the point of suggesting he come along, but her message has gotten through to him, and he simply nods acknowledgment. A curtain descends between them.

Rio stands on legs and feet that have gone pins-and-needles and heads for the door. And there, in her path, stands Gwenllian.

'I'm just going to catch some air,' Rio says. 'All this cigarette smoke.'

Gwenllian says, 'There will be another.'

'Another . . . what?' Rio asks, but Gwenllian has already drifted away, moving with silent grace as if the feet concealed below her long dress barely touch the floor.

Outside it is darkest night, cold but without a hint of wind so that the cold burns her exposed flesh but does not cut through her coat. Rio glances up and sees that the overcast cloud is breaking up, revealing brilliant stars.

She decides to walk around the inn, hoping to get the circulation going in her feet. And she's curious about the other side of the inn, which must front a road, surely. Though just as surely the door to the inn should be on the road side, which it is not. Then again, Rio tells herself, foreigners do things differently.

But when she walks around the side of the inn she finds no road there, either. The inn seems to sit in the middle of nowhere special, out in the middle of the endless sea of wet grass. Does everyone who comes here arrive on foot? Then there must surely be a village nearby. She looks in every direction, expecting to see some faint light, even a tiny village must have some light showing. But no.

'They got cold beer in there?'

The voice makes her jump. It's directly behind her and she spins, wishing she had brought her rifle. She tenses, ready to use the few personal combat skills she recalls from Camp Maron.

The man is a surprise in every way. He's wearing a uniform, but not like any she's seen before. It's some sort of camouflage, but all in shades of brown and beige. There's a stenciled name tag on his chest that reads 'Charles,' and beneath the camouflage cloth there's something stiff, like a strange, concealed coat of armor.

But the most surprising thing is that he is a colored man, a negro.

He is not the first negro Rio has ever seen. There had been a negro camp across a stream from Camp Maron, and she had passed a humid hour with a young colored woman from . . . well, Rio can't recall from where. Not the first colored person Rio has met, but still Rio finds him strange, almost impossible. He's a large man, very fit, and the casual confidence in his gaze confirms to her that the lieutenant's bars on his uniform are the real thing.

'Who are you?' Rio asks, straining to keep her voice level.

The colored man offers a thin smile. 'Lieutenant Dick Charles. I'm number three.'

A chill that is not from the cold air travels up Rio's spine.

'And I have to ask: are you simply unaware, Private, that you are required to salute a superior officer?'

The voice is unquestionably American, tinged with an East Coast accent she cannot quite place. New Jersey? Brooklyn? She gulps, stiffens to attention and snaps a salute. The negro officer returns her salute.

'Sorry, sir,' Rio says.

'Not a problem, soldier. Tell the truth, I'm not sure you are required to salute a dead officer.'

'A . . .'

The lieutenant tilts his head and gives her a look very like Cole's sometimes bemused expression. 'It's 1942, Richlin, but I'm wearing desert camo and body armor, and I'm a black officer. While you are wearing a regulation World War Two era uniform. That suggests the situation is a bit . . . unusual . . . wouldn't you say?'

'This is a dream, isn't it?' Rio asks, adding a belated, 'Sir.'

'A dream . . . a nightmare . . . a visitation . . . take your pick. According to my orders you will have been briefed by two others, a British corporal and a Russian partisan.' There's a slight curl of distaste when he says 'Russian'.

Rio nods and manages to whisper a shaky, 'Yes, sir. They were . . . disturbing.'

'Roger that,' Lieutenant Charles says with a sudden wide grin. 'The ghost of war past, that'd be George Fisher. And the ghost of war present, young Tatiana who died just about an hour ago. Can you get your head around that, Private?'

'Sir?'

'Do you read me? I'm asking if you catch my drift?'

Rio frowns. 'Yes? Sir?'

'War past, war present, and now me: war future.'

Rio looks around, feeling a little desperate, though oddly less afraid. The lieutenant has an easygoing manner, despite his rank. And though it's hard to say much for sure based on two minutes of conversation, he also doesn't seem at all concerned that she's a woman.

'What war, sir, if I can ask?'

'Not "can I ask," Private, it's "may I ask." No one doubts your ability to pose a question, just the propriety of doing so.'

Rio almost giggles – almost, but not quite – since he sounds suddenly like her English teacher back home.

'You may ask, Richlin, but I may not answer. I won't pretend I'm clear on the physics of the supernatural, I have not been read in on that subject. In fact I'll admit this is all a bit odd.' He looks around, sighs, nods. 'For example, I'll be damned if I recall actually being briefed on any of this, yet I do seem to have some clear notions, among which is that you are Private Rio Richlin, and I am not to give dates or details. I think what we have here is a case of not messing with the past or the future may go FUBAR.'

Rio gasps. 'You say FUBAR in . . . your war?' She has only recently learned the all-purpose acronym which in a slightly more polite version stands for Fouled Up Beyond All Recognition.

'Hell, Private, all war is FUBAR. It was FUBAR back in 1402, during the Glyndŵr rising when the Welsh made a play for independence from England.'

'Sir, is that Glyndŵr with a little hat on the 'w?"

'It is,' he answers. 'There was a course on it at

the Point. Well, not just on that, the curriculum covered a number of failed uprisings.'

'That's the name of this inn, sir.'

Lieutenant Charles looks past her at the inn and nods. 'I suppose it would be.'

'Can I . . . May I ask whether the name Gwenllian means anything to you, Lieutenant?'

'Gwenllian of Wales? That was before the whole Glyndŵr rising by a couple centuries, if I recall. She was heiress to the Welsh throne so Edward Longshanks had her locked up in a nunnery for more than five decades.'

Rio feels a shiver, but it comes with a surge of pity. To be locked away for more than fifty years . . .

Lieutenant Charles stamps his feet as if keeping them warm. 'I suppose I'd best get on with my story. Let's go inside.'

He leads the way inside, then stops. 'Jesus, Richlin, do you people ever stop smoking?' He waves a hand at the cigarette smoke. 'Those things kill you, you know. Emphysema, lung cancer.' Then he shrugs. 'Of course that isn't so much a concern for me, is it?'

'Sir?'

Charles walks on past a snoring Cassel, past a softly singing Cat, past Jack who glances up at Rio and says,

'Still gloomy out there?' If he sees Lieutenant Charles he shows no sign of it.

'It's clearing a little,' Rio says. She indicates the area she's occupied and the American takes the seat previously occupied by the Brit and the Russian. The ancient publican shuffles over carrying a tall beer which he sets down in front of the lieutenant as though the colored man – no, *black* is how he referred to himself – is a regular.

'Outstanding.' Charles takes a long pull on the beer. 'I'm no great storyteller, so here goes nothing. I was on my second deployment up at a FOB – Forward Operating Base – way out on the bleeding edge. There was a haji village not a click away. Old guys and their goats, women – although you never actually saw them of course. And kids. The young men all off with the Taliban or running opium or whatever. Far as we knew we were on good terms with the village head man. We helped fix their well, and some special forces folks gave them all polio shots and –'

'Polio shots?' Rio asks, frowning.

'After your time,' Lieutenant Charles says with a dismissive wave. 'Hell, all this is after your time, the war, the technology, all of it. But just play along, and you'll make sense of it.'

'Yes, sir.'

'Anyway, we're feeling snug as bugs in a rug in our FOB. We've got decent cover, a hole to piss in, all the MREs you can gag down, and it's about 120 degrees in the shade, with no damn shade. We patrol through the village and up into the hills a bit, but Taliban ain't gonna be caught by us, that's for damn sure, they know every rock, every gully, and have done for generations going back to the days of Alexander.'

'The Great, sir?'

'There's really only one Alexander that gets the single name treatment, Richlin.'

'Yes, sir.'

'So I sent Sergeant MacAvoy's squad out on patrol because the eye-in-the-sky thinks they see activity. I figure it's just a file of goats wandering around, or maybe some of the boys in the opium trade making a market run. MacAvoy's a good sergeant, conscientious, on her third deployment so she knows what's what. The ROE – Rules of Engagement – at that point call for us not to engage directly with Taliban patrols if we can avoid it but to call in an air strike. Which between you and me is bull because up in those gorges all the Hellfires do is make the rubble bounce. You want to kill haji, you gotta get down and dirty with him.'

He frowns and looks more closely at Rio. 'Here's the thing, soldier: if you just sort of relax and let yourself go with the flow, this'll work better.'

'Go with the flow, sir?'

'Relax. Close your eyes. Stop trying to make sense of it. I am here to deliver a lesson to you, Richlin.'

'Why me, sir?'

'You have a friend with connections.'

'A friend?'

'Maybe family. Someone wants you to get an education pronto.'

Rio stares at him for too long. He returns her gaze with a bit of a twinkle in his eye, a man who knows more than he will tell. And even in a dream Private Rio Richlin is not going to cross-examine an officer.

Rio decides to try and 'go with the flow,' which strikes her as an interesting and useful phrase. She eases back in her seat and closes her eyes. Then she opens them, astonished. For just a moment she'd been somewhere *very* different. For a moment she'd been climbing a murderously steep, rocky hill, in stifling heat, beneath a dropping but still blistering sun.

'See?' Lieutenant Charles says. 'Told you.'

So Rio closes her eyes again, figuring she might as well get this over with as quickly as possible.

She is the third person in a six-soldier squad. A large negro . . . black . . . woman walks with the familiar vigilance of a soldier walking point, keeping a steady pace while her tan camouflage helmet turns left, right and up the slope, like a metronome, left, right, up.

Behind her a white man is her mirror image, looking where she isn't, her opposite, looking left when she looks right. Their weapons seem fragile, as if made of something like gray Bakelite, but still conveying a distinct sense of menace.

The woman on point raises a hand, makes a fist, and the soldier behind her immediately stops and drops to one knee. He has his strange rifle raised and is scanning the world around him through its sights. The soldiers behind Rio do the same, very professional, very smooth – very much unlike her own squad.

'What you got, Merrick?' To Rio's astonishment, the question is coming from her. *She* is Sergeant MacAvoy. Her eyes fly open.

Charles wags a finger at her, side to side. 'Unh unh. That's cheating.'

Rio closes her eyes again and the woman she's called Merrick whispers, 'Movement at two o'clock. See that bush? Back of there, maybe a point left.'

Rio draws out a pair of binoculars she did not know she had. She raises them and trains them on the spot. Then she keys the switch on her radio and gives the proper call sign and seconds later is speaking – magically it seems to her – to Lieutenant Charles.

'Looks like we got a possible ambush, LT.' She draws a strange device from her belt, pushes a small button and sees a line of numbers which she reads off. 'We're uphill of the ville.'

'Roger that,' comes Charles' voice.

The situation is immediately clear to Rio. They are uphill from the village. If Charles calls in an air strike it's likely to send a few thousand tons of rock tumbling down onto the village. Which, she reminds herself, is a definite no-no. Not to mention the fact that there are women, children and old men in the village, and no sign of Taliban.

Whoever *they* are.

'Bring it back in,' comes the lieutenant's voice and Rio is just about to transmit that order when she hears a whoosh, spots a trail of smoke and yells, 'Incoming!'

The squad drops. The RPG – which she somehow knows means Rocket Propelled Grenade – explodes behind the squad. Seconds behind the explosion comes rifle fire, pinging off the rocks.

'Return fire!' Rio yells and suddenly she sees just what these seemingly fragile rifles can do. She squeezes off short bursts, feeling almost no recoil and watches bullets raise sparks around a bearded head which quickly ducks behind cover.

'Okay, pull back. Merrick! Bring it back.'

But Merrick does not answer.

'Merrick!'

'She's hit, Sarge!' comes a controlled but distressed cry from Private Marlow. Merrick and Marlow. M&M. They're buddies.

Rio curses – something she simply does *not* do – and begins crawling forward, sharp stones stabbing her elbows, but she's been equipped with a sort of pad, like a football players' pad, that protects her elbows, and matching devices on her knees.

She crawls past Marlow who is red in the face and wild-eyed. 'Put some fire on them, Marlow,' Rio snaps, and crawls past. She reaches Merrick, who is clutching at a leg wound.

'How you doin', Merrick?'

Merrick, with a great deal of cursing, says she's shot in the leg.

'Lie flat, I'll put a compress on it.' Rio fumbles in her belt and produces the bandage which she wraps with practiced movements around the blood-stained leg. Then Merrick jerks as a second bullet finds her other leg and she cries out in pain.

'I'm a pull you back,' Rio yells, excited, keyed up and angry but not yet afraid. This is not her – MacAvoy's – first fight. She grabs handfuls of Merrick's uniform blouse and drags her back as Merrick yells in pain, and now Marlow is there, the three of them wedged between sharp rocks, hands fumbling, all three of them cursing, and suddenly Marlow slumps.

'What the –' Rio demands, before realizing that a chunk of Marlow's face is on the ground beside her, a bloody chunk of meat. She looks at Marlow and sees that a bullet has gone through his head. He is dead.

'Marlow!' Merrick screams, clawing at him, while Rio fights panic and struggles to pull Merrick back and a second RPG comes screaming in and explodes.

The world spins, a rock tumbler, like being in the back of a cement mixer everything going around and around. She feels herself sinking. A vast black curtain is being drawn around her, as if she is on a stage and taking a final bow, but not ready to bow, not ready for the curtain.

Unconsciousness.

Rio opens her eyes. 'Does she die?' she asks Lieutenant Charles.

He hesitates before answering. 'Not just yet,' he says grimly. 'Not just yet.'

Rio closes her eyes again and opens them as MacAvoy. Her first sensation is a pounding headache. Then comes thirst.

She is hanging from her wrists. Cords have cut deep into the flesh. She can no longer feel her hands, but every other part of her is throbbing with pain.

There is a spindly tripod a half dozen feet away. It holds what must surely be some sort of camera. Three bearded men in turbans stand to one side, smoking, rifles slung over their shoulders.

A fourth man, younger, chubby, with a less impressive beard, stands just beside her, also facing the camera. He is speaking a language she does not understand. Declaiming loudly, passionately.

In his hand is a long, curved knife.

Rio wants to shout, wants to scream, but her lips are thick, and she feels holes where some of her teeth should be, and her nose is clogged with dried blood.

Then the loud-voiced younger man moves behind her. He grabs her hair in one fist and yanks her head back.

Rio opens her eyes. 'No. I don't want to . . . I don't . . .'
She is clammy with sweat. Her heart is racing. She feels
the urge to vomit.

There is no question in her mind what happened –
will some day happen – to Sergeant MacAvoy.

'No,' Charles says softly. 'And I didn't want to see
it, either. We caught the courier carrying the video to
wherever the hell they broadcast from. We stopped it.
So MacAvoy's parents never saw it, thank God. Thank
God for small mercies. But I did.'

He sighs. 'I liked MacAvoy. She was army all the way
through. Good with the men. Brave. Tough.' He shakes
his head, no longer meeting Rio's eyes. 'But I did see
it. I saw it in living color. I couldn't stop myself.' He
looks away, seeing things that Rio does not even want
to imagine. 'Yeah. I saw it.'

Rio is silent, waiting, hoping it's over.

'You want to know what I did, Richlin? I lost it,
that's what I did. I called in a mission. I told them the
village had been overrun. I called in a mission on
the village.'

'A . . . a mission?'

'Air strike,' he explains. 'In my time, see, air strikes
are capable of great precision. An F-16 floats way
up there, and it gets a call on the radio, and it drops

a bomb or fires a smart missile, and the target goes . . . poof.' He makes a gesture with his hand, a slow-motion explosion.

'MacAvoy was one of mine, see. I'd lost a man on my last deployment, and . . . well . . . I guess you always blame yourself. I'd had to meet that man's wife back in North Carolina. I met his kids. And I didn't want to have to do that ever again. I did not want to have to look your husband – sorry, I mean MacAvoy's husband – in the eye and admit . . .' He sighs and there is a thready, shaky sound. 'She had a daughter.

'So I lost it. I lost it. I called in the strike. And when it was over they wanted a BDA – a bomb damage assessment. So I had to walk out there to that village. And of course it was destroyed. The bombs we have, the missiles we have, well, they are very fine examples of what science and technology can do when it comes to killing.

'Rubble was all that was left. Hell, the village wasn't much to start with, just half a dozen homes, a little poured concrete mosque no bigger than a garage. All of it blown to hell. Some of the men had been out working, tending their animals or whatever the hell, so it was mostly women. And kids. Little dead children. There was this one boy, not a year older

77

than my own son, and his head . . . his arm was . . .'

He breathes hard, like a man who might start yelling. Or crying.

'Yeah,' he says softly. 'Nine dead. And not a damned one of them Taliban or Al Qaeda, just poor-as-dirt kids . . . Anyway. So it was covered up, but they sent me home on a psych. PTSD. Post Traumatic Stress Disorder they said, but that wasn't it, Richlin. The shrink kept saying it was the heat of battle. But it wasn't. I wasn't confused. I knew what I was doing. I was getting revenge. I was getting some payback.

'People would come up to me, civilians, you know, and say, "thank you for your service." And . . .'

His voice chokes. Rio watches his throat convulse. She sees tears in his eyes. It is several minutes before he can go on.

'I'm thinking, God no. Don't thank me. Thank MacAvoy. Thank Marlow. Merrick. Thank all the guys who did not lose it. You know? Not me. Do not thank me for killing nine civilians.'

He brushes at his eyes, then smoothes a hand back over his close-cropped skull.

'Long story short, I started hitting the bottle. I couldn't tell anyone. Not my wife, what would she . . . How would she ever . . . Not the shrinks at the VA – you know, the Veterans Administration. It never happened, you see, all covered up, nice and neat. But every night when I closed my eyes there was that little boy . . . But the anger was still there, too: I hated them, what they did to MacAvoy. I hated all of them, every lousy one of them. I even hated that little boy.

'My marriage broke up. My wife took our son and moved to Colorado. It was on the two-year anniversary of MacAvoy's death. I drank most of a bottle of very fine Scotch, see, I knew what was coming. I knew what I had to do. I had my personal weapon, my nine mil.'

He mimes cocking an automatic handgun.

He opens his mouth and mimes putting the barrel between his lips.

He mimes pulling the trigger.

And now, for the first time, Rio sees the gore atop his head.

Rio wants to say something. But she has no words for this.

'Yeah. And then . . . then, I was here,' Charles says with a crooked smile. 'And I'm supposed to be teaching you something.'

Rio shakes her head in horror. 'I don't know what to say.' She does not add 'Sir.' It seems irrelevant now.

This is not an army officer, this is a man speaking to her from the lowest level of his own personal hell.

'I am your final cautionary tale, Richlin. The ghost of wars future. And I suppose what I have to tell you comes down to a single word.'

'What word?' Rio whispers.

Charles thinks about it, eyes down, then finally raises his face and says, 'Forgiveness.'

'Forgiveness? For the people who did that to Sergeant MacAvoy?'

'Yes,' Charles says. 'Not because you love them. Not for *them* at all. For myself. For yourself, when it's your time. You can't forgive yourself, see, unless you can also find a way to forgive them.'

He nods as if finally realizing something. He makes a wry grin. 'You don't want to wait till you're dead to figure things out, Richlin.'

'You hated them.'

'I did.'

'But . . . the other one, the Russian girl, she said you have to hate.'

'I suppose you do,' Charles says, not meeting her eyes. 'It's a lousy business. You hate because if you don't hate you can't kill, and if you can't kill, you die. But eventually war comes to an end. Eventually, if you survive, you will need to put it behind you. You'll need to forgive. Them . . . and yourself. It's the only way to ever go home.'

'I want to go home,' Rio admits, sounding like a lost child. Then she looks sharply at Charles. 'Do I, sir? Do I go home?'

Lieutenant Charles makes a wry grin and pushes back from the table. 'Now that, soldier, is not something I can tell you.'

'Why me, sir? Why am I being visited like this? You started to tell me.'

'Well, Richlin, you got someone looking out for you.'

Rio looks past the officer and sees Gwenllian across the room. The girl is solemn, but her gaze is kind. Lieutenant Charles rises, turns and walks toward the door, and as he walks George Fisher appears and falls in step with him. And behind them, Tatiana.

The three walk in single file past Gwenllian, who is no longer red of hair, no longer just someone who reminds Rio of her sister. She is Rio's sister.

Rachel Richlin stands in her Navy uniform. She is soaking wet. The water of the Pacific ocean drains from her, forming a puddle.

Rachel salutes Lieutenant Charles who returns the courtesy. George gives her a wave, enlisted soldier to enlisted soldier. Then Tatiana who simply says, 'Comrade' and walks by.

And finally Rachel looks at her sister.

Rachel stiffens, brings her heels together, and raises a rigid salute to Rio.

6

Rio wakes when Jack shakes her gently. 'Hello, old girl, the fog has thinned a bit and Sarge wants to get going.'

Rio looks around her, owlish. The squad is packing up, groaning and grumbling as usual.

'All right, people, saddle up,' Cole says.

The room has changed. The bar and the tables and the chairs are all the same, but there is electric light, and the man behind the bar is a cheerful-looking young fellow. There's a war poster on the wall warning that Careless Talk Costs Lives.

Rio hefts her rucksack and slings her rifle over her shoulder.

'You all right?' Jack asks.

'Fine, Stafford,' she says.

He begins to help her settle the pack on her back, but she steps back. The signal is clear enough for Jack to understand it. There is to be no gallantry between them.

His expression is surprise, settling into understanding. He's a smart young man, Jack Stafford. Rio decides he'll make a fine soldier. Maybe they all will.

Though probably not Jillion Magraff, who has wrapped a discarded tablecloth around her bootless foot.

'Interesting,' Rio mutters.

Jenou overhears her. 'Interesting? Sleep?'

'War,' Rio says softly.

'What do you know about war, Richlin?' Geer asks with a derisive snort as they head out through the door, out to the road that Rio could have sworn was not there the night before.

Rio is on the verge of giving him a one- or two-word brush-off, but the smart-aleck in her is subdued at the moment. 'Well, Geer,' she says, 'I guess I know three things.'

'Three huh?'

'Three. Some day you're going to have to forgive the enemy. And yourself.'

'I'm not forgiving a damn –' Geer starts.

'Shut up, Geer,' Cole says. 'Go on, Richlin.'

Outside at last the air is fresh and there is even a tiny – and no doubt temporary – glimpse of sun.

Everything, everywhere is green. Including, of course, Rio's squad.

'Okay, I guess what I think . . . what I know right now . . . is that some day you'll have to forgive, in the meantime . . . I don't even feel right saying this. My mother would . . .' She shakes off the feeling that her mother is watching her. She doesn't really want her mother watching her. 'I guess number two is that, like the old shooting instructor back at Camp Moron said: I'll have to learn to . . . you know . . . to hate them.'

Rio frowns and wants almost to laugh. It feels very wrong, somehow. But not incorrect. It makes something inside her squirm.

Cole says, 'Okay, first off, we don't know we're going anywhere near the front. Any front. Ever.'

'But we are, Sarge,' Rio says flatly.

Cole looks at her, his expression unreadable. His voice is quieter when he says, 'So what's number three, Richlin?'

'Actually . . . It was number one,' Rio says.

'Yeah?'

'It was that you don't have to like the people in your squad. You don't even have to be able to stand the people in your unit. But.'

'Yeah?'

'But I guess as long as you wear the same uniform, they're your brothers and sisters.'

Sergeant Cole takes a moment to relight his cigar. He looks at Geer and says, 'You figure that sounds right, Geer?'

Geer, to Rio's surprise, frowns thoughtfully. She can practically hear the sarcasm coming. But then Geer nods.

'Reckon it does, Sarge,' Geer says.

'Yeah,' Cole says, satisfied. 'Yep. That *is* number one.' He gives Rio a long look through the smoke of his cigar, and nods very slightly. Then, 'Okay, people, we still got an OB-jective. Richlin take point, Geer on her back. Right?'

Rio and Geer both nod.

'Oh,' Cole says with a sudden grin.' 'And Merry Christmas to all.'

From the back of the column comes Jillion Magraff. 'And God bless us, everyone.'

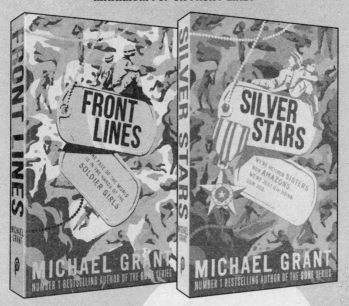

Discover the number one bestselling series from

MICHAEL GRANT

THE **GONE** SERIES

MICHAEL GRANT
NUMBER ONE BESTSELLING AUTHOR

A WORLD WITHOUT ADULTS...

A small town in southern California: In the blink of an eye everyone over the age of 15 disappears. Cut off from the outside world, those that are left are trapped, and there's no help on the way. Chaos rules the streets.

Now a new world order is rising and, even scarier, some survivors have power – mutant power that no one has ever seen before...

MORE IN THE SERIES...

"I love these books"
Stephen King

LOOK OUT FOR
GONE SPIN-OFF SERIES

MONSTER

COMING
AUTUMN 2017

About the author

Michael Grant is the evil genius of Young Adult Fiction. Among his biggest fans is Stephen King who called the *GONE* series 'A driving, torrential narrative'. Michael's life has been similarly driving and torrential. He's lived in almost 50 different homes in 14 US states, and moved in with his wife, Katherine Applegate, after knowing her less than 24 hours.

Michael and Katherine were running their own cleaning business when they wrote their first book. Since trading in his Marigolds, Michael has now written around 150 books – with Katherine, as himself, under pseudonyms and as a ghostwriter.

He now lives in the San Francisco Bay area taking inspiration from the charming view of Alcatraz. From across those dark waters have emerged his dystopian fantasy series, *GONE*, his thrilling futuristic trilogy *BZRK*, and the menacing *Messenger of Fear* books.

Now he is reinventing history with *Front Lines* and *Silver Stars*. *Dead of Night* is a previously unseen episode that takes place during the timespan of the first book, and has been written exclusively by Michael Grant for World Book Day 2017.

Read on for a thrilling extract from . . .

I HAVE NO
SECRETS

PENNY JOELSON

A stunning new novel coming in May 2017

I tense as soon as I hear the doorbell. I know it's him. I know it's Dan. Sarah's still upstairs getting ready and I hope she comes down soon. I don't want him coming in here.

Mum calls up to Sarah and I hear her say she'll be down in a tick. 'We've been keeping her busy, I'm afraid,' Mum tells Dan, 'so she hasn't had much time to get ready!'

'Ah, I know she wouldn't have it any other way,' says Dan. 'She's a diamond – and you too. What you do for these kids.'

I listen to them chatting away and Mum laughing at Dan's jokes. Everyone loves Dan. Then Mum says she must get back to the kitchen, she's left things on the stove and she's sure Sarah will be down soon.

It's quiet for a moment. I hear the distant clattering of pans in the kitchen. Then I hear Dan's voice, coming closer as he speaks.

'What are you watching then? Ah – *Pointless*!'

I tense. I can hear him breathing. Then he whispers, 'Bit like your life, eh, Jemma?'

He's standing behind me now, but I can't see him because my wheelchair is facing the TV. I try to focus on the quiz questions and forget he's there but he gives a long, dramatic sigh.

'Don't know how you can bear it.' His voice is low, not loud enough to be overheard. 'Watching the telly must be the most excitement you get.' He only speaks like this when no one else is around. He used to ignore me completely, but not any more.

He moves so he is in front of me, blocking my view of the TV. Grimacing, he leans forwards. I get a gulping feeling, a tightness in my throat.

'If I were you, I'd top myself,' he whispers.

My heart thuds as he rubs his head thoughtfully.

'Oh, yeah – you can't, can you? Listen,' he continues, 'if you ever want a bit of help, I could . . .'

We both hear footsteps on the stairs. Dan backs away. His face transforms from ugly sneer to fake grin, his features softening as if they have been remoulded.

'I'd have done better than that pair!' he laughs, pointing to the telly. 'Reckon we should go on this, eh, Sarah?'

I get a waft of Sarah's perfume, which is quickly overtaken by the smell of onions frying in the kitchen.

'I'm useless at quizzes,' she laughs, as she comes into view. 'I bet Jemma could do it, though, if she had the chance.'

I don't know about that, although I do sometimes get the right answers. It's possible I'd be better than

Sarah. She's a brilliant carer, but she's not too clever when it comes to general knowledge – or boyfriends.

At the outside edge of my vision, I see her kiss Dan softly on the lips.

Watching them, my own mouth feels suddenly dry.

The pair playing *Pointless* are out. They look very disappointed.

Dan and Sarah only have eyes for each other. 'Ready?' Dan smiles at Sarah. 'You look stunning, babe.'

She nods and turns to me. Her eyes are sparkly, her cheeks flushed. 'Bye Jem. See you in the morning.'

'See you Jemma,' says Dan. He winks at me.

I have no secrets of my own. I've never done anything without someone knowing about it. I'm fourteen years old and I have severe cerebral palsy. I am quadriplegic, which means I can't control my arms or legs – or anything else. I can't eat by myself. I can't go to the loo without help. I can't move without someone lifting me with a hoist or pushing me in a wheelchair. I also can't speak.

I've been this way all my life. I can see though, and I can hear, and sometimes people forget that. They don't realise that I have a functioning brain. Sometimes people talk about me as if I'm not even there. I hate that.

And sometimes people tell me their secrets. I think it's because it's quite hard to hold a one-way conversation. If they are alone with me, they want to talk to pass the time and they end up telling me stuff. They know I won't tell anyone else so they think telling me is safe. The perfect listener.

Sarah told me her secret. She's cheating on Dan. She's still seeing Richard, her old boyfriend, because he's so sweet and she can't bear to hurt him by breaking up with him. Neither of them knows the other exists.

I'm always worried when Sarah has a boyfriend, although I enjoy the way she gossips to me about them. She has this dream of a fairytale wedding – she's even shown me pictures of her ideal wedding dress online. I know I should want her to be happy – and I do. It's just that I'd miss her so much if she went off to get married. She's the best carer I've had.

Anyway, I don't want her to marry someone who isn't good enough for her. And I definitely don't want her going off to marry Dan.

Sarah's in a great mood when she's back on duty the next morning, though I can tell she's got a hangover and is trying to hide it. She's drinking loads of coffee. She clearly had a good evening with Dan and is singing a track by our favourite band, Glowlight.

She's wheeling me from my bedroom to the kitchen when I hear the clunk of post landing on the mat. Sarah stops to pick it up and puts the small pile of letters on the kitchen table.

'Oh look – one for you, Jemma,' she comments.

As she pushes me into my place, I see my name on the top letter – parents/guardians of Jemma Shaw. I rarely get post. I wonder what it could be?

Mum picks up the pile and glances down. Then she quickly moves my letter to the bottom and puts them all on the kitchen counter. Sarah doesn't seem to notice.

Now I am even more curious. Why doesn't Mum want to open it?

After breakfast Dad gets up to leave for work. Mum follows him out into the hallway to kiss him goodbye. Their voices are muffled, but I can pick out Mum's words. She says, 'There's been another letter. I haven't read it yet, but I think we'll have to tell her.'

I strain to hear Dad's reply. 'Yes – she is family. Jemma has a right to know.'

Family? What are they talking about? If only I could ask. It sounds like they're planning to tell me. I just have to hope that they do.

Dad's gone and Sarah's in the kitchen with me, easing my arms gently into my coat, ready for school. I'm conscious that my letter is still there, at the bottom of the pile on the counter.

Olivia's moaning that she can't find her reading book.

Mum sighs. 'When did you last have it, Olivia?'

Olivia shrugs. 'Dunno.'

'Have a look in your bedroom, will you?' Mum tells her.

Olivia slopes off slowly towards the stairs.

'Sarah, can you go with her? I can't see it down here.'

'Sure,' says Sarah. You're ready, Jemma. That's one down at least!' She hurries off after Olivia.

'Where's Finn's water bottle?' Mum mutters to herself. 'I'm sure I washed it yesterday. I bet you know where I put it, Jemma.'

As it happens, I do know. I saw it fall off the draining board and down behind the bin.

The doorbell rings and Mum wheels me towards the door. We never know if it will be my minibus or Finn's cab that comes first. Today it's the cab that takes Finn to his special school.

Mum sighs and pushes a spare green water bottle

into Finn's bag, which is not going to please Finn as he always has the blue one. She helps him with his coat and gives his hair a quick comb. He wriggles away as fast as he can and out the front door with his taxi escort, Jo.

'Reading book found,' Sarah says, coming down the stairs.

'I hope you said thank you, Olivia?' says Mum, though she knows full well that Olivia hasn't.

'It wasn't me who lost it, Lorraine!' Olivia protests. 'Why do you always have a go at me? It's not my fault!'

She stamps her feet and I'm relieved when the doorbell rings again so I can leave before Olivia starts screaming.

As the minibus jolts along the road, I think about the letter and try to work out what Mum and Dad were talking about. Family? Mum has an aunt and Dad has a brother, but we don't see much of them as they live a long way from here. Were they talking about their family? Or . . . or could it be mine – like my natural mum, the one who gave birth to me and then dumped me? Could she have finally decided she wants to see me?

I hope it's not her. I don't want to see her – not ever!

She probably only wants to get a look at me and gawp. I hope Mum and Dad tell her to get lost.

As soon as Dad is back in the evening I wait for them to talk to me – but they don't say anything. Sarah isn't being chatty like she normally is, so I don't have anything to distract me from thinking about the letter. Though I guess it means she's not talking about Dan so much. I can almost start to pretend he doesn't exist.

Right now Sarah isn't talking at all – she's concentrating as she battles to get my rebellious arms into the sleeves of a jumper. My muscle spasms are worse than usual because I've not been sleeping well. Thinking about Dan has been keeping me awake.

'Tonight's the night,' she whispers. I wonder what she means. She's not seeing Dan again, is she? She's seeing so much of him I'm scared sometimes that she's going to run off with him! But of course, she'd never do that.

'I'm splitting with Richard,' she says. 'It has to be done – I'm not being fair to him.' She runs a brush quickly but gently through my short tangly hair. 'I can't keep putting it off. I know he'll be gutted, though – he's such a softy.'

At last Sarah is doing the right thing. It's no good

going out with someone just because you feel sorry for them. Now she just needs to dump Dan too! I wish she had more sense with men. She's had a few boyfriends since she's been here and they've all been hopeless. Like Jason, who was always borrowing money from her and never giving it back, and a guy called Mario who was only interested in football and a total bore. Next was wimpy Richard. And then Dan came along.

Sarah's getting ready to go out when the doorbell rings. She's meeting Richard in town, so I know it's not him. I'm in the living room, but the door's open and for once I'm at an angle where I can see into the hall. Dad opens the front door. I hear Dan's voice.

What's *he* doing here? Sarah is definitely not expecting him.

Dad invites Dan in and I hear the front door shut. I can hear them talking, but I can't take anything in. When Dan sees Sarah all dressed up, what's he going to think? He'll get suspicious for sure. I strain to listen, but now Olivia's started one of her tantrums. She's lying on the floor somewhere behind me, kicking and screaming like a two year old except twice as loud.

I hear Dad call upstairs, 'Sarah! Dan's here!'

He's assumed Sarah's going out with Dan!

At least he's warned her – it would be awful if she

came down and just found Dan in the hall. I have no idea what she's going to do.

Thankfully Dan doesn't come into the living room – I think Olivia's screaming has put him off. Mum comes in to see what's up with her, saying a quick hello to Dan as she passes. She turns my wheelchair round, which is annoying as I'd rather watch what's happening in the hall than look at Olivia, who is lying on the floor at the far end of the room, pointing and screaming. Now I can see what's upset her. One of her ballet shoes is trapped on the candelabra light fitting, near the ceiling. Finn must have thrown it up there. He's got a good aim.

Mum calms Olivia and says Dad will get it down. Finn is nowhere to be seen. Mum turns me to face the TV and switches it on. Then she pulls Olivia up gently, hugging her, and holds her hand to lead her out. I hear them going upstairs.

I'm conscious that Dan is still in the hall. Sarah calls to say she'll be down in a few minutes. Then I hear Dan sigh. He walks into the room and goes straight to the telly and picks up the remote, flicking through channels. He's acting as if I'm not even here. I wish I could say 'Oi! I was watching that!', even though I wasn't really.

He settles on the news. I don't want the news. On the screen I can see a coffin being carried into a church. A reporter is speaking. It's only when I hear him say the name Ryan Blake, that I start paying attention properly.

Ryan – from down the road. It was his funeral today. I'm interested now. I want to know what the police have found out. Mum and Dad think Ryan might have been into drugs.

'Police are still appealing for witnesses,' the reporter continues, 'and his parents are pleading for anyone who knows anything to come forward.'

Dan suddenly turns towards me.

'You don't know anything . . . do you, our Jemma?' he sniggers.

The worst thing isn't his joke about me being thick – it's that he calls me 'our Jemma'. Like he's part of the family or something.

'Here's a secret for you,' he continues, 'and I know you won't go telling anyone.' He winks. There's a pause. He presses his face close to mine, so close I can feel his hot breath on my cheeks.

'They're never gonna catch me!' he whispers, nodding at the screen. He stands back, smiling as if he's gloating. 'There's something for you to chew on, *freak*!'

Sarah's feet patter on the stairs.

Dan backs off and flicks the channel quickly over to a game show.

Catch him? What does he mean?

It's a wind up – it must be . . .

'Hiya babe,' he says.

'What are you doing here?' Sarah asks. I see her arms flapping a bit like Finn. I can tell she's panicking, but she's also gazing longingly into Dan's eyes. She won't cancel on Richard to go out with Dan, will she?

'You left a glove in my car,' he tells her. 'I only found it today. I was passing so I thought I'd pop it in. Don't want you getting chilly fingers!'

'Oh – thanks! I was wondering where it was,' she replies. 'But I've got to get a move on. I'm off out with Emma and Rihanna – we're going to the cinema.'

'Out again?' he says.

'It's Emma's birthday,' Sarah says quickly. 'We're having a girls' night out. Becks is coming too. We're seeing that film you said was for soppy teenage girls.'

Sarah seems to have her excuse ready prepared – but I guess this is what she's told Mum too.

'No way!'

'Yeah, really,' Sarah laughs for a little too long. 'And I must go or I'll be late.'

'No worries – I'll give you a lift,' says Dan.

'No, Dan. I'm fine,' Sarah assures him.

'It's no prob,' says Dan.

'Oh . . . All right then.'

An uneasy feeling grips my chest. I don't want her to go with him. What he said to me . . . Surely he was joking. Dan's horrible, but he wouldn't actually kill someone. Would he?

Sarah says goodbye to me and touches my hand gently. Her hand is hot – she knows this is a mess and she briefly meets my eyes with a knowing glance before turning to the door.

'Bye Jemma,' Dan says, winking. I see his sneering face in my head when he called me *freak* and remember what else he said. I don't trust him one bit.

And the way he turned up here – it doesn't feel right. Maybe she's done something to make him suspicious. Was he trying to catch her out?

They go and I hear the front door bang shut.

Dad comes in and stares up at the ballet shoe on the light fitting, muttering, 'you've got to be joking,' under his breath.

HIGH VOLTAGE
YA READING FROM
ELECTRIC MONKEY

EUGENE LAMBERT

THE SIGN OF ONE

ONE FOR SORROW, TWO FOR DEATH

Huntley Fitzpatrick

MY LIFE NEXT DOOR

A perfect summer. A secret love.

BORN SCARED

KEVIN BROOKS

WINNER OF THE CILIP CARNEGIE MEDAL

LYNN WEINGARTEN

SUICIDE NOTES FROM BEAUTIFUL GIRLS

LISA HEATHFIELD

CAN YOU PAPER FLY WITH BUTTER BROKEN FLIES WINGS?

ELIZABETH WEIN

CODE NAME Verity

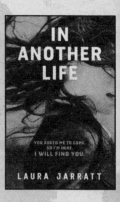

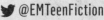
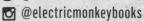

HAPPY BIRTHDAY WORLD BOOK DAY!

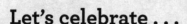

Let's celebrate . . .

Can you believe this year is our **20th birthday** – and thanks to you, as well as our amazing authors, illustrators, booksellers, librarians and teachers, there's SO much to celebrate!

Did you know that since WORLD BOOK DAY began in 1997, we've given away over **275 million book tokens**? WOW! We're delighted to have brought so many books directly into the hands of millions of children and young people just like you, with a gigantic assortment of fun activities and events and resources and quizzes and dressing-up and games too – we've even broken a **Guinness World Record**!

Whether you love discovering books that make you **laugh**, CRY, *hide under the covers* or **drive your imagination wild**, with WORLD BOOK DAY, there's always something for everyone to choose–as well as ideas for exciting new books to try at bookshops, libraries and schools everywhere.

And as a small charity, we couldn't do it without a lot of help from our friends in the publishing industry and our brilliant sponsor, NATIONAL BOOK TOKENS. Hip-hip hooray to them and three cheers to you, our readers and everyone else who has joined us over the last 20 years to make WORLD BOOK DAY happen.

Happy Birthday to us – and happy reading to you!

SPONSORED BY

#WorldBookDay20

BOOK IN
FOR YOUR NEW ADVENTURE TODAY

CELEBRATING

WORLD BOOK DAY

20

2 MARCH 2017

3 brilliant ways to continue YOUR reading adventure

1 VISIT YOUR LOCAL BOOKSHOP

Your go-to destination for awesome reading recommendations and events with your favourite authors and illustrators.

 Booksellers.org.uk/ bookshopsearch

2 JOIN YOUR LOCAL LIBRARY

Browse and borrow from a huge selection of books, get expert ideas of what to read next, and take part in wonderful family reading activities – all for FREE!

 Findalibrary.co.uk

3 DISCOVER A WORLD OF STORIES ONLINE

32 podcasts to try

Stuck for ideas of what to read next? Plug yourself in to our brilliant new podcast library! Sample a world of amazing books, brought to life by amazing storytellers. **worldbookday.com**